I'm
a
Bendy Gymnast

Written by Charlotte Sabin
Illustrated by Andy Wegg

ISBN

978-1981603435

FOR
Amber

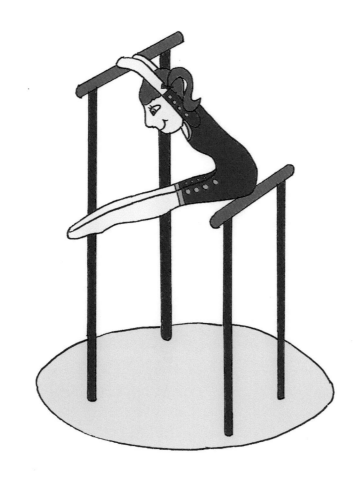

This book belongs to

....

I'm a bendy gymnast, Amber is my name.

Playing dressing up, is all part of my game.

Joe and Maddie are watching, my pug Toby too.

Watch closely and take notes, so you can copy too.

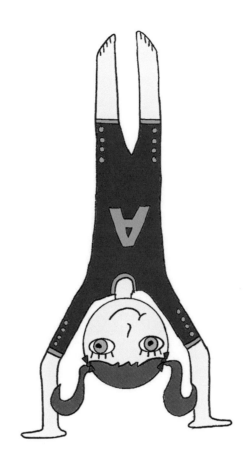

This is called the 'Handstand', place your hands on the floor

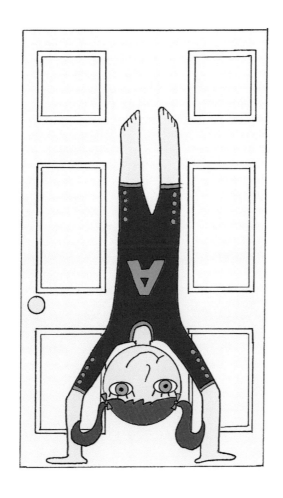

And push off with your feet; if you need to use a door.

This one is very tricky, pretend you're a wheel.

Stretch out your arms and legs, this is
how you do the 'Cartwheel.'

Pretend your a crab, lying on the sand.

Push up with your body, your legs and your hands.

Jump up and down on your bed, pretending it's a trampoline.

Throw your arms above your head
and...scream!

Give yourself lots of room when doing
the roly poly.

Put your head between your legs, just look at Toby...

Being a gymnast is lots of fun, you can fit into the smallest of spaces.

But it can also cause you to pull the
funniest of faces.

The End

Other books in the Playing Dressing Up Picture Book Series

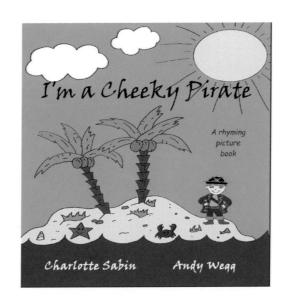

Join James on his pirate adventure.
ISBN 9781981357994

Join Hannah as she puts on a ballet show for her family.

ISBN 9781514191606

COMING SOON

I'm
a
Scary Ghost

25288309R00016

Printed in Poland
by Amazon Fulfillment
Poland Sp. z o.o., Wrocław